CROSSROADS

VOLUME 2

N.L. MCLAUGHLIN

TWISTED SKY

For my Family

Lorelai -

In German folklore, Lorelei is the name of a beautiful siren or mermaid who is said to sit on a rock in the Rhine River, singing a hypnotic song.

THURISAZ

CHAPTER 1

"SHH, SHH, SHH," she whispered as she swept a soft finger over his sweat soaked forehead.

He whimpered and tried to speak, his lips pulling against the tight stitches that held them closed.

"There, there, there," she cooed. "I'm doing you a favor." A subtle grin played across her lips. "Just think, you'll never have to worry about getting old. You'll always be remembered as the hot, handsome young man you are today."

Tears streamed out of the corners of his eyes.

Lori sat up and gazed down at him. "Don't worry, this won't take very long," she said, twirling a curly lock of his thick brown hair around her finger. "You'll be sleeping forever soon enough."

"Please," he forced through the stitches, followed by uncontrollable sobs. Tears and snot ran down both sides of his face.

As she stared down at him, a profound hatred welled up inside her. Men such as these never owned up to the hurt and suffering they inflicted. It was always the woman's fault. She was asking for it. She knew what she was getting into. She liked it. Life was too short to settle down with one woman.

It was always the same.

His arms bound behind him by zip ties, he thrashed beneath her, his body twisting in a desperate struggle.

Lori smiled. "Now, now, there's no use." She laughed. "You're not my first, and you certainly won't be my last."

He made a grunting noise; his eyes flashed with hatred and rage.

"There it is." She leaned close enough for their lips to brush together. "That's the way I want to remember you."

In a final desperate attempt, he thrust his head forward, slamming into her mouth, splitting her bottom lip.

Lori pulled away and wiped the blood from her chin, then sat up and grinned. "Do you know what happens when someone gets a belly wound?" She pulled a bowie knife from the sheath attached to the back of her belt and held it up, spinning the tip against her finger as the waning sunlight glinted against the polished blade. "The movies got it all wrong. Truth is that belly wounds are the worst kind of wound a person can suffer. They're painful, almost always deadly, and they smell horrible." She giggled and gazed down at him. "Do you know why that is?"

His body shook with silent sobs, each breath hitching as he struggled, and failed, to pull free of his restraints.

She waited for him to calm—to accept his fate, then, with a gleeful chuckle, she plunged the blade into his belly. The cold, smooth steel met little resistance as it sank into his flesh, a warm wetness blooming around the wound. The metallic scent of fresh blood filled the air. Once again, she leaned down and kissed him on the cheek. Slowly, she twisted the blade and dragged it across his abdomen, hearing the squishy, wet sound of flesh tearing. It was music to her ears.

He gasped and sputtered, coughing up blood that oozed out between the stitches.

She pulled the blade free, then wiped it off on his t-shirt and put it away.

After a last stroke of his hair, Lori climbed out of the box and gazed down at the growing crimson stain in the middle of his body. She could already smell the feces escaping from his intestines where she stood. She held a hand above her eyes, nose crinkled, and gazed skyward. Two carrion eaters had already been summoned. She watched them soar overhead, their shadows dancing on the ground below as they gracefully circled, patiently waiting for their next meal. But this was not meant to be theirs.

Her lips curled into a cruel, malevolent grin as she gazed down at him one last time before slamming the lid shut, immediately triggering a barrage of hysterical screams from the man inside.

Whistling her latest melody, she covered the box with the rocky soil, pausing now and then to tap out the beat. If only she was better at lyrics, she thought. This tune was catchy. Alas, her drumming was far more impressive than her poetry; her rhythms were infectious, while her words lacked flair.

With a final sigh, she stepped back and surveyed her handiwork. Silence surrounded her, she couldn't help but wonder when the man's screams subsided. Did he grow silent on his own or was the earth piled above him muffling the sound? With a dismissive shrug, she spun around and sauntered her way through the field of unmarked graves and back to her truck that sat idle in the gravel driveway.

The shovel landed with a thud in the truck bed; she

brushed the dirt from her hands, a faint scent of earth clinging to them, before glancing at her watch. There was just enough time for her to shower and maybe catch a quick nap before heading in for her shift at the bar.

With the sun slowly waning in the sky, she climbed behind the steering wheel, she told herself that one day, she would be the drummer of a world-renowned band. She would be famous and rich. People all over the world that she didn't know would adore her. Smiling over the images that danced in her mind, she turned out onto the road and drove back into the city.

CHAPTER 2

THE TINY HOUSE stood dark among the backdrop of warmly lit, cozy cottages. Such a stark contrast to the neighbors—to the place she knew as a child.

Gravel crunched under her tires as she rolled into the driveway, stopping in front of the garage. Too small to accommodate any vehicle she had ever seen; it was the perfect size to be a sound studio.

Mr. T., short for Mr. Tinkles, the neighborhood stray, was already there, a shadow moving silently around her feet, his amber eyes gleaming. She leaned down and scooped him up, noting the tiny black satin cape that was secured around his neck as though he was a superhero. "What's up little guy?"

A deep, rumbling purr vibrated through her hands as the cat nestled against her.

"Looks like the neighborhood kids got a hold of you again," she said, scratching under his chin. "You're gonna have to do your nightly patrols without this." She unclasped the cape. "We don't want you getting stuck anywhere."

As though that was all he wanted from her, Mr. T. squirmed and wriggled until she let him drop to the ground. With a final meow and a flick of his tail, the cat darted through the fragrant purple and pink hydrangea bushes, vanishing into the shadows.

With the tiny cape still in her hand, she climbed the back stairs and entered the house from the side door to the kitchen.

A heavy, oppressive silence hung in the air, broken only by the occasional drip of water from the kitchen sink. Like everything in her life these days, it was drab and lifeless. She didn't bother to turn on a light, there was no need, she could wander through the house blindfolded and never bump into anything. After a momentary pause at the fridge, to grab herself a cold beer, she strolled over to the entry to the living room and leaned against the door frame.

For a long time, the entire room was in desperate need a complete makeover. With the dark, heavy wood paneling, the threadbare, stained carpet clinging to the floor, and the chipped, decaying furniture, it was an overwhelming task to decide where to even begin. Her eyes took in the room; so many precious childhood memories were tied to every corner of this time capsule. That was the true reason she refused to do any sort of remodel. She wanted to hold tight to the last vestige of a life long gone.

A wistful smile touched her lips as she remembered the nights snuggled safely on her handsome daddy's lap while he read her stories about princesses and magical realms. Her Meemaw was always ready afterward with warm milk and chocolate chip cookies, a comforting end to the day.

She could almost hear the old man, her Papaw, pleading with the old woman for some cookies of his own. But Meemaw insisted the cookies were for the young ones.

With a shared glance, Lori and her dad exchanged conspiratorial grins as they munched on their bedtime snack.

Back then, the world was vibrant and alive. Every day was filled with laughter and love. Yes, the house was tiny and cramped, and money was not to be wasted on frivolous things, but for young Lori, they were better than wealthy—they were happy.

She never knew her mother, the woman had disappeared shortly after Lori was born, leaving her father, Jesse, to raise her alone. At eighteen, he was still very much a child himself, but he was determined to raise his daughter as best as he could. With the help of his parents, Meemaw and Papaw, he did pretty well.

With its creaky floors and paint-chipped walls, the cozy, little two-bedroom house in the quiet Texoma town held some of her fondest memories. In her eyes, her father, with his kind smile and twinkling eyes, was the most handsome man on earth. Her grandparents doted on her, always more than willing to watch her while her father worked long shifts at the garage.

Papaw was a wealth of old stories and strange knowledge, while Meemaw was all about the proper way for a young lady to carry herself, mixed here and there with just the right amount of Texas, country girl, defiance.

Every night, young Lori would wait until Jesse came home, tired and smelling of oil, metal, and grease. He would scoop her up effortlessly, her small body light as a feather in his arms, and carry her to the warmly lit living room, where she'd curl up on his lap as he read a bedtime story.

Saturdays were her favorite time. That is, if her father didn't have to work.

During the warmer months, the day would start with an

early morning stop at the local bait shop, followed by a stop at the local food truck for a breakfast burrito so huge and delicious, filled with savory potatoes and melted cheese, that she could never finish it.

With their fishing gear in hand, they walked along the pebbled banks of the lake, the cool morning breeze on their faces, to their favorite spot to set up their poles. There they would sit, feeling the warmth of the rising sun on their skin, the glistening water reflecting the dawn's colors as they watched the horizon ignite with vivid orange and yellow.

Afternoons involved a quick, simple lunch at home; then, it was off to the local park, where the sounds of children playing filled the air as Jesse chased her, pretending to be a growling monster chasing a beautiful princess. She would laugh so much, by the time it was time to go home, her tummy would hurt.

They could always count on a warm, hearty dinner when they arrived home. The little family would sit around the table and talk about everything and nothing at all.

After dinner, she and her father would go outside to the tiny garage where his drum kit was set up and he would play along to various songs. When she was very small, she would sit on his lap as he played, sensing the bounce of each beat. Sometimes, he would hand her a drumstick and let her tap along. By the time Lori was six years old, he had already taught her to play, or as he would say, she would take over the kit and play. He insisted she was born to be a great drummer—calling her his little metronome.

A tear slid down her cheek.

With one long drink, Lori finished her beer, then spun around and snatched another ice-cold one from the fridge. The night was still young, and she had at least two hours before her shift. There was plenty of time to shower, but right now she needed to burn off some steam.

Her drum kit was calling her. Time to lose herself in music. She quickly grabbed a couple more beers, then made her way outside to the tiny studio.

CHAPTER 3

A THICK HAZE of stale alcohol and sweat filled the air, making the already tedious work seem to drag on at a snail's pace, as the hours crept by. Though the pay was pitiful—the work was so underwhelming, it gave Lori plenty of time to focus on other pursuits, which is why she stuck around. Having inherited the house and the land, she didn't need a lot of money to live.

After popping the tops off another round of cheap beers for a group of local linemen, she rested her hands on the sticky bar top, taking in the scene. The laughter, the smell of sweat and grime, and the general air of rowdiness meshed perfectly with the old rock tune playing over the speakers.

It was a typical, mundane Wednesday. Of course, the day of the week hardly mattered, this seedy little dive wasn't exactly considered a local hot spot. She preferred it that way. Less temptation.

Two regulars, engrossed in their game, leaned over the pool tables, the rhythmic click of the balls a steady backdrop to their friendly competition. She knew them only by the nicknames she'd given them—Sparky, for his slim stature and energetic personality, and Tank, because the man was an absolute giant. The duo came in almost every night after work to play a few rounds of pool and drink a couple of beers. She had no desire to know them beyond that.

With nothing left to clean and no fresh drinks to serve, she pulled out her phone and opened the dating app.

So many prospects, she mused, as she flipped through the endless parade of smiling faces. Blond, brunette or ginger, that was really the only difference between them.

With a subtle ping, a message popped up on her screen. For the past couple of days, she had been chatting with a man named Jack. Things were going well, in fact, they were heating up quite nicely.

And, right on que, here he was, inviting her for a drink. She smiled and tapped a response.

```
Jack:   Hey   gorgeous,   sorry   if   I'm
interrupting  you  at  work,  I  just  couldn't
stop thinking about you.
```

Of course you couldn't, she thought. This was all a part of the hunt. Put on her best impersonation of a slightly naïve, horny woman and reel them in. It was too easy. After waiting the proper amount of time, she tapped out a response.

```
Lori:  Oh  yeah?  What  were  you  thinking
about?
```

.   .   .

He responded immediately.

Jack: I want to meet up. You name the place
and time; I just have to see you in person.

She shook her head and chuckled lightly as she pictured him taking his place among her collection. If only he knew how much danger he was in. But these sorts of men, blinded by lust and overflowing with self-confidence, never considered that. In their minds, they were apex predators, and women were simply innocent, unsuspecting creatures ripe for the taking. Oh well, he would soon find out how wrong he was about that.

With a tap of her finger, she opened the map app on her phone and searched for a bar in Dallas. It had to be somewhere understated yet trendy, a balance between sophisticated ambiance and bustling crowds for easy anonymity. A place where they could blend in, unnoticed.

After locating the perfect little place, she messaged back and waited for his response. It took him less than thirty seconds to reply enthusiastically.

Her plans set, she closed her phone and peered up at the clock then sighed. She still had four hours left to her shift. Sparky and Tank's game was still going strong over by the pool table, their playful banter accompanied by the satisfying *thunk* of the balls, while the linemen, a boisterous bunch, signaled her for another round.

CHAPTER 4

THE DRINK WAS STRONG. Ordinarily she would approve, but, in this instance, the overuse of vodka threw the flavor off. As a bartender herself, Lori had a hard time enjoying the way other's mixed drinks. It seemed like a simple task—liquor plus flavors—but she was surprised by the difficulty in finding someone who could balance the ingredients in order to create a good tasting drink that was also strong.

She glanced down at her phone. Nine twenty-five—her date should arrive any minute. Across the table, the drink she ordered for him sat, its colors reflecting in the dim light of the room. A tall Jameson and coke, that was what he said he preferred to drink. Simple, she liked that. Even his name was simple—Jack.

She cast her eyes around the room, observing the various couples, musing on the probability that many of them had met online through the app. After all, online dating was all the rage these days. It made hunting simple.

It never really took much. A few suggestive comments and some innocent flirting soon spiraled into an overwhelming urge to meet in person. Their pretense of wanting a true relationship was a carefully constructed charade designed to manipulate her, a charade which she, in turn, pretended to believe.

The vibrantly lit bar was alive with activity. So many pathetic people—both men and women of varying ages, all working in their own ways to do whatever it took to not go home alone. The men made a show of their supposed wealth and achievements hoping to impress, while the women, using far too much makeup and shapewear, tried to attract their attention.

These places and the people who attended them were all the same. Whether it was in a seedy dive bar like the one she worked in up in Gainesville, or this one, with its trendy music, bougie atmosphere and expensive drinks—that were hardly worth the price. The major distinction between her bar and other, more trendy establishments lay in the behavior of the patrons; in her seedy little dive, they felt no need to maintain appearances or put on a pretense of wealth and beauty. Here, everyone was performing. It was funny how the illusion of money could bring out the most ridiculous behavior.

She just didn't understand it. Maybe it was due to the way she was raised; maybe it was simply because she was broken inside. Whatever the cause, she had no desire whatsoever to play courting games. In her opinion, it was all a waste of time. Contrary to all the romantic literature and popular movies, the existence of a knight in shining armor was nothing but a myth. No one was going to come and save you from the drudgery of normal life. There was no such thing as authentic, sincere, and unwavering love; it did not exist.

Flirtatious laughter erupted, cutting through the din of

small talk and old rock music. Lori's focus turned to a slender, blonde woman who occupied a barstool beside a handsome blond man. With their heads close together, they playfully teased and toyed with one another.

A creepy sensation washed over her, the unsettling feeling that someone was watching her. She slowly scanned the bar until her eyes landed on a peculiar man in the far corner who was sitting alone. His dark sunglasses obscured his eyes, making it impossible for her to know for sure if the intense gaze she felt was actually coming from him.

How strange to be wearing sunglasses indoors at night, she thought.

With a slight tilt of his head, a mischievous grin curled the corners of his lips as he raised his drink, offering a silent toast in her direction.

Was that meant for her? She carefully scanned her surroundings, her eyes darting from left to right, and concluded that she was right. The toast he had raised was intended solely for her. Feeling a bit confused, she returned her gaze to the bar only to find that the strange man was no longer there.

Had she imagined it? A single empty glass, perched precariously on the bar, served as undeniable proof of his having been there just moments before. But where could he have gone so quickly?

A familiar song played over the speakers. Lost in the rhythm, Lori closed her eyes, her finger tapping in time with the music, her mind awash in cherished memories of her father's infectious enthusiasm as they played along to this song together.

Her mind's eye played the images like a faded movie reel, the scenes unfurling one after the other, each one as vivid and detailed as if it were projected onto a silver screen. Those were such happy times. Why couldn't it have stayed that way?

Like a needle scratching across a record, the screen in her mind suddenly and abruptly changed, instantly altering the mood. The happy young man who doted on his daughter was gone, replaced by a haggard, weary-eyed older man, worn down and exhausted by the relentless demands of a life gone wrong. The eyes of a man whose gaze upon his child revealed only profound disappointment.

The song ended. With a heavy sigh, Lori opened her eyes, actively pushing away the profound sadness that threatened to engulf her completely. Those days were long past, it was best to leave them in their peaceful grave.

She glanced up at the door just in time to see her date enter. The moment his gaze met hers, a charming smile spread across his face, and with immediate purpose, he swiftly moved toward her.

"Sorry I'm late," he said as he slid into the seat opposite her.

Checking her phone, Lori saw that he was only a minute late for their meeting. Flashing a demure smile, she said, "I'll try not to hold it against you." She gestured to his drink. "I ordered you one, hopefully the ice didn't water it down too much. Though with the heavy hand this bartender uses to mix his drinks, I doubt it'll make much of a difference."

He took a tentative sip, followed by a wince of clear discomfort, then let out a dramatic, loud exhalation. "Whoo! That is strong." He took another drink, then leaned his elbows on the table. "So, we finally meet in person. I know this is something you likely hear a lot, but I truly mean it when I say you are absolutely stunning."

With a look of practiced innocence, she gazed back at

him. "You're not so bad yourself, Jack. It's a wonder you haven't been snapped up yet."

It was time for her to perform. The events of the next hour would decide the course of the evening. She had to be on her best behavior. Staring across the table at him, a deep sense of loathing burned in her belly. There were many men like him, all of them users, as common as a dime a dozen. Nothing more than dogs who changed partners quickly, with little consideration in between. In their eyes, women were dehumanized to the point of being viewed as nothing more than vessels for their physical gratification, with no regard for anything else.

Keeping her eye on the end goal, she leaned forward and put on her best performance.

CHAPTER 5

THE EVENING COULDN'T HAVE GONE any better. The events unfolded exactly as though they were following a script she had written herself. The ease with which men could be manipulated never failed to amaze her; this was especially true if they believed they were pulling the strings themselves.

She had to give Jack credit; he was certainly putting forth his best performance. One could almost believe he truly was interested in her as a human being as opposed to nothing more than a warm body to rub up against until he was satisfied.

Nearly two hours passed before he finally broached the subject of leaving the noisy bar in favor of a more quiet and private location.

"I thought you would never ask," she said enthusiastically. She meant this with every fiber of her being.

Lori knew better than to leave the bar with her date. It was far too easy to track. She always had them walk her to her vehicle where they would share their first kiss. After that, they drove separate vehicles to their final destination.

After a quick check to make sure she had all the tools she needed, she put her truck in drive and sped out onto the street, following her unwitting prey.

Music blasting over her new, high-end sound system, her mind filled with images of what was to come. With her meager salary from the seedy little dive bar, it was quite a stretch financially to have such an expensive system installed. But she never splurged on herself, so she counted this as money well-spent.

The city was silent all around them. Bathed in the glow of the tall streetlamps, with the occasional flash of red, yellow or green, like out of season Christmas lights.

Jack, driving his flashy sports car, sped ahead of her, deliberately slowing down at intervals to keep his car beside hers.

She played along. Smiling coyly back at him as he flirted from the safety of his vehicle.

Time and again, she found herself marveling at the striking similarities that connected all these men. It was a phenomenon that never failed to amaze her. It was almost as though somewhere out there a machine was printing them out, one by one. Or perhaps there was there a 'how to' book out there somewhere. Or some sort of training camp.

No, they were born this way. How else could one explain the teen boys like Colter?

A red-hot, searing wave of hatred threatened to consume her completely; it was a reaction that came with the mere thought of him. The fact that he was probably living it up, playing his games, continuing to deceive and hurt women, filled her with such rage that she wanted to track him down online, and inflict a gruesome, personal revenge. She fantasized about skinning him alive and adding his remains to the collection of trophies that she kept.

Her lips curled into a wicked little grin as she indulged in a cruel fantasy; the look of sheer terror in his eyes, giving way to pathetic moans, followed by desperate pleas for mercy. Of course, there would be none. After all, he showed no mercy when he violated her trust and ruined her life for nothing more than internet likes and follows.

The memories of that night were a constant in the back of her mind. A silent movie playing over and over. It served as a perpetual, unwelcome reminder of the worst moment in her life. The moment that changed everything forever.

Just thinking about her naivete made her cringe. If she closed her eyes, she was still able to see the reflection of herself in the mirror as she prepared for that fateful date. How could she be so stupid? She had everything a girl could want; popularity, a close group of friends, and a bright future ahead of her. She didn't need him. Yet, in her own stupidity, she allowed herself to feel like a stupid schoolgirl when Colter Trask, one of the coolest boys in school, asked her to go out with him. She had a crush on him for so long; it was like a dream come true.

Her young teenage mind swirled with images of the loving couple they would be. Holding hands in the hallway, sneaking the occasional kiss between classes, homecoming and prom. Of course, they would be crowned king and queen.

Her dad would be so happy for her and proud.

Of course, that's not even close to the way it all played out. There was no hand holding or innocent cuddles, nor was there prom—at least not for her.

Following Jack through the dark city streets, an ominous cloud settled over her. Yes, these sorts of men were a scourge on the planet. She was doing a service to all women. One less fuck boy to deal with. A world without their deceptive lies and manipulative tactics would be a significantly improved and more positive place. No more fake smiles and flirtatious behavior, no more empty promises, and no more heartache and pain upon realizing they were lying the whole time.

Her mind flashed back to the face of the boy who first stole her heart then smashed it into pieces. Had she never trusted him, her life would have never taken the turn it did.

CHAPTER 6

COLTER TRASK. To this day, just thinking about the name sent a current of white-hot rage through her body.

How could she have been so naïve? Better yet, how could he be such a monster?

At sixteen, Lori had everything going for her. However, like most girls her age, she was painfully inexperienced when it came to matters of the heart. Raised on a steady diet of fairy tales with handsome princes and beautiful ladies, she was woefully unprepared for reality. The only experience she had with men was through her father and Papaw, and both of them were nothing like Colter. But she had no way of knowing that at the time.

In her eyes, Colter was sweet and adorable. The way she felt, a mixture of excitement and nervousness, every time he looked at her and smiled, sent shivers down her spine. She was completely infatuated with him. For many weeks, she would steal glances at him, quickly turning away whenever he noticed her looking. She memorized his mannerisms and the funny way he spoke with his country boy drawl.

He was, by no means, the most popular boy at school, but he held his own among the crowd. Unlike a lot of boys their age, he didn't seem to feel the need to kiss up to any of the older, more popular kids. He was simply Colter. A sweet, country boy with a mischievous wink in his eye and a sideways smile.

She spent her days at school, quietly pining away over him. After school, she would go home and spend hours imagining him falling head over heels in love with her.

The day he asked her out was like a dream.

It was a Wednesday. Lori remembered that because it also happened to be the band's practice day at school. Her friend, Jaimie had been hinting all day that something special was gonna happen, but she never really delved into specifics. As the hours ticked by without any sort of revelation, Lori let it go and chalked it up to another instance of her best friend falling for gossip.

The day had ended. As the final bell rang, the majority of her classmates excitedly gathered their belongings and prepared to leave for the day. Lori however, remained behind, searching the depths of her locker for a battered and aged set of drumsticks. Her newest pair were left at home earlier that morning. Had she known it would be this difficult to find the old pair in her locker, she would have gone home during lunch to retrieve them.

"Finally!" she muttered under her breath, then stood straight and slammed the thin metal door closed only to find herself face to face with Colter.

Her mouth suddenly dry, she choked, "Hey."

He smiled. "Hey, back."

A paralyzing silence filled the air as the most uncomfortable seconds of her life ticked by. Why was he just standing there?

"Are you joining us today?" came a deep male voice.

Lori glanced over to find Mr. Whitehouse, the music teacher, standing in the hallway. "Um, yes!" Sorry!" was all she could say, then she turned her gaze back to Colter.

Before she could say anything, he blurted out, "Are you going to Dylan's party this weekend?"

Dylan was having a party? He was one of the most popular senior boys in the school. That must have been the secret Jamie was referring to all day.

She stood in place, struggling to formulate an explanation as to why she wasn't going, that didn't make her sound like a loser. Before she could stop herself, the truth rolled off her tongue, "I didn't know he was having a party. I guess the list hasn't made the rounds yet." In her head, she berated herself for saying something that sounded so pathetic.

"Well, now you know," said Colter. "I'd really like it if you came and hung out with me."

Shock coursed through her body. Unable to move or speak, she stood there, staring back at him like a fool.

"What do you say?" he asked.

"I-I don't know where he lives." Inside she rolled her eyes and berated herself for such a stupid answer.

"Don't worry about that," he said. "I'll give you a ride."

Her mind exploded. All her daydreams and thoughts about him danced around in a wild kaleidoscope of vivid images that even she was unable to parse. What do I do? What do I say? Is he asking me out?

Her heart pounded as though it was ready to burst right out of her chest.

"Come on," he said. "Don't leave me hangin', say yes."

"Yes!" she blurted mindlessly. "I'll go."

"Cool!" he said loudly. "Why don't you give me your number."

"My number?"

"Um yeah," he grinned. "Your phone number. I kinda need it if I'm gonna pick you up." A serious look swept across his face. "You do wanna go with me, don't you?"

"I do!" she said quickly. "I-I'm sorry, you just caught me off guard." She tucked a lock of hair behind her ear and fumbled to get her phone out of her pocket. With sweaty palms, she swiped the tiny screen.

"Here, lemme," he said as he took the device out of her hands and began typing. A second later, his phone chimed. He pulled it out, glanced down at his screen. "We'll chat later."

"Ahem," said Mr. Whitehouse, now tapping his toes with his arms crossed.

"Okay," she replied with a nod. "I get home around six."

Colter nodded. "Sounds good." He peeked over his shoulder at the teacher, then turned back to her. "You better go before he kicks you out of the band."

She giggled. "He couldn't do that. He'd never find another drummer." Her moment of bravado quickly faded to embarrassment over the brag, but Colter seemed unfazed.

He handed her phone back to her and winked. "I'll catch ya later," he said, then with a final nod of his head, he moved past her and down the corridor.

At the other end of the hallway, Mr. Whitehouse coughed and cleared his throat.

Her phone buzzed in her hand. She glanced down and saw that Colter had sent her a message.


```
Knock 'em dead. We'll chat later.
```

. . .

It chimed a second time.

`You're pretty when you smile.`

Her heart soared as she stared down at the words, at first refusing to believe they said what she thought they said. I'm pretty. He said I'm pretty. Feeling as light as a snowflake, she made her way to the band room for practice.

Giddy and on cloud nine, she worked her way through band practice and somehow managed to get home, though she hardly remembered any of it.

When supper rolled around, she kept her phone tucked away in her pocket, set to silent, anxiously awaiting a message. She was so preoccupied, even Meemaw made a comment.

Throughout the evening, she waited for a text that didn't come. Gradually, her elation gave way to disappointment. She went to bed early that night, feeling saddened in a way she had never felt before.

Sometime around eleven o'clock, her phone awakened her with a chime.

`Colter: Sorry I didn't message earlier. I got busy with chores. How was your night?`

She stared at the screen unsure whether she should respond right away or wait a moment or two first. In the end, she couldn't contain herself.

. . .

Lori: It's okay. I had chores and stuff too. It's late.

Colter: You want me to leave you alone so you can sleep?

Lori: I didn't say that. We can chat for a while.

That night, the two teens stayed up until the first signs of dawn, passing messages back and forth. They compared musical tastes and talked about their favorite movies.

When morning came and it was time to go to school, Lori was so tired, she worried she might fall asleep mid-day. Her fears were quickly set aside when she got to school and found Colter waiting by her locker, smiling wildly.

They were virtually inseparable for the next two days. Between every class, he was there with that adorable smile of his. He even spent lunch alone with her under the giant oak tree where she would sometimes sit alone to read.

At night, they would chat via text, sharing thoughts and dreams with one another.

Lori was in love.

When Saturday rolled around, she was absolutely ecstatic. Feeling a little too shy to share the news about Colter with her dad and Meemaw, she decided to keep her secret to herself. When they asked her what she was doing, she responded by saying that she was going to a party with her friends. She told herself it wasn't really a lie, her friends would be there. After a few cursory warnings about being careful, she waved goodbye and left the house, heading toward the library where she met Colter.

The vibrations from the music inside the house made the air reverberate to the beat, as though it were a living, breathing entity. With his hand in hers, Colter guided her through the crowd to the kitchen where his friends had gathered.

To this day, the single most vivid memory of that night was the warm sensation that tingled throughout her body as she held his hand.

CHAPTER 7

SHE ROLLED to a stop in front of a traffic light and slid her gaze over to Jack who was idling in the vehicle next to her. A coy smile played on her lips as she leaned from her window.

"I was just thinking," she said.

"Yeah?" he asked. "About what?"

"You wanna do something fun?"

He grinned foolishly and nodded his head up and down.

"Let's go sit under the stars."

"The stars? Like outside?"

It was her turn to nod her head. "I have some ranch land about forty minutes from here. It's such a beautiful night, it would be perfect to sit on a cozy blanket, sip some wine and see what happens." She gestured behind her. "As luck would have it, I just so happen to have a bottle of wine and a blanket in the back."

"Just happen to have, huh?" he said, grinning. "I'm in," he said without hesitation. "But why don't you hop on into my car and we can drive together."

"Or," she replied. "Why don't you park your car and come ride with me? After all, I'm the one who knows how to get there. And," she giggled, "my truck will handle the country roads a lot better than your sports car. As awesome as it is." She flashed a coy smile. "Don't worry, I'll bring you back home before dawn."

He revved his engine. "Sounds like a plan," he said.

As soon as the light changed to green, Jack immediately turned left, his car speeding down a vacant street to reach the municipal parking lot. As Lori waited patiently along the street, he parked his car and locked it securely, then he jogged quickly over to her vehicle before finally climbing into the passenger seat. As soon as he closed his door, she leaned over and kissed him, just to cement the deal.

The drive out of the city was full of small talk and flirtatious banter. Much to her surprise, she was enjoying herself. Jack had a wonderful sense of humor. Too bad it wasn't enough to save him.

Approaching midnight, she arrived at the iron gate and brought her truck to a stop.

"Wow!" said Jack, gazing out at the rolling landscape. "You own this?"

"I do. My grandparents bought it before I was born, hoping to build their retirement home on it. My Papaw died way before they could pull it off." She shrugged. "My dad never managed to scrape together the money or time to do anything with it, so when my Meemaw passed, I inherited it all."

She punched the security code into the keypad and watched as the gate slid open.

"So, you think you'll build something on it one day?" asked Jack.

They rolled past the gate and down the long gravel

driveway. "I don't know," she said. "Maybe. Right now, I just use it for hunting and recreation."

"Recreation, huh?" he grinned. "Am I to understand that I'm not the first man you brought out here?"

She rolled to a stop alongside a small shed and turned off the engine. Lori reached over and caressed his jaw with her finger. "A lady never tells. Come on," she said, then climbed out of the vehicle.

The night was calm, with a warm breeze. Overhead, the sky was littered with millions of glittery stars.

Jack whistled. "You weren't kidding. It's nice out here." He scanned the rolling hills that surrounded them. "I still can't believe you own all this?"

"Uh, huh," she made her way to the back of the truck and lowered the tailgate.

"You weren't kidding, you really came prepared," he said as he opened the cooler and pulled out a bottle of wine and two glasses.

She guided him to the weathered shed, where two rocking chairs sat silently on the small porch.

A symphony of chirps and croaks filled the night as crickets and frogs called out from the undergrowth all around them.

With a gentle pour, Lori filled two glasses with crisp white wine, then handed one to Jack before sitting down to gaze at the tranquil view.

"To a memorable night," she said as she lifted her glass.

"To a memorable night," he repeated.

She watched with a keen eye as Jack took a large drink of his wine, all the while pretending to do the same. Based on his size, she speculated he might need to drink the entire glass in order to get the full effect of the drugs.

Twice, he tried to kiss her, but she rebuffed him,

insisting that it would be wasteful to not finish their wine first.

When he finished his glass, he climbed to his feet and held out a hand for her. She could tell by the way he swayed, the drugs were taking effect, so she went along with his prompting. He led her over to the blanket that they placed on a soft, grassy spot, then spun around and kissed her.

His body swayed against hers. He pulled away and raised a hand to his head. Staring at her in confusion, he staggered, then fell to his knees. "I'm not feeling—," he muttered. An angry look flashed across his face. He glared up at her and said, "You bitch! What did you do?"

He clambered to his feet, his movements clumsy and urgent, and launched himself at her, sending her sprawling to the ground, the impact jarring her head and making her see spots.

He pressed his body against hers, pinning her in place, his hands like iron bands around her neck. A low growl rumbled in his chest, a vibration she felt through her whole body.

This wasn't how it was supposed to be; a bitter taste filled her mouth as she processed the events. Crushed beneath his weight, she clawed at his face and hands with one hand. Meanwhile, with her other, she frantically reached out for a weapon: a rock, a stick, anything.

Her fingers brushed against the cool glass of the wine bottle. With a renewed sense of resolve, the bottle whistled through the air as she brought it down with all her strength, striking him on the side of the head with a loud, dull thud.

His body stiffened, then collapsed on top of her.

Lori lay there for a moment as she tried to catch her

breath. She struggled to breathe, his suffocating weight pressing down, stealing the air from her lungs. She had to get out from under him. Muttering angrily, she squirmed and strained, wishing she'd used a stronger dose of the drug. The thought of being smothered, pinned beneath him, struck her as so ironic it made her giggle.

After several minutes of struggling, her muscles burning from the exertion, she was finally free. She climbed to her feet and brushed herself off. "Nice try, asshole," she said aloud, then, just for good measure, she leveled a kick to the center of his abdomen.

Time was of the essence. She had no idea how long he would remain unconscious, so the first thing she had to do was tie him up. She pulled her hair up into a bun, then whistling one of her favorite songs, she spun around and retrieved her supplies from the shed.

Usually, she savored each moment, taking her time to enjoy the details. It made it far more enjoyable that way. But on this occasion, she needed to work quickly, her heart pounding in her chest as she moved.

First, she bound his hands and feet tightly, ensuring that even if he woke, he'd be unable to move. Next, with swift, practiced movements, she stitched his lips closed; the needle glinting in the dim light. Nothing ruined the mood faster than hearing their pathetic cries for help. At last, using the makeshift litter she'd prepared, she pulled his weight across the uneven field toward her secret garden. There, with aching muscles, she lowered him into his box and into the grave she had dug the day before.

Then she waited.

The sun was peeking on the horizon when he finally opened his eyes. A wave of panic washed over him. He thrashed against the restraints, his breath coming in ragged gasps. A muffled scream wracked his body as he struggled, unable to open his mouth, his eyes wide with pain and terror.

She climbed into the box and straddled him, reveling in the sensation of him bucking beneath her.

"You can struggle and try to scream, but it'll do you no good," she said calmly. "This is your end. You might want to welcome it with some dignity."

A sharp cry escaped his lips as he pulled against the stitches. A tiny trickle of blood ran down along his jaw from a small tear.

She kissed him on the forehead. "I would say this won't take long, but we both know that would be a lie." She giggled. "They say it takes three days for a man to die of dehydration, so I suppose you can count on maybe being alive that long." She climbed out of the box and gazed down at him. "I will say you gave me a run for my money. Which is why you earned a few extra days."

"Don't worry," she said, tapping a finger on the lid. "I installed a hole for air, so at least you won't suffocate."

His eyes, filled with a desperate, frantic panic, darted around as he bucked and moaned, a thin stream of sweat beading on his brow.

Lori blew him a final kiss, then said, "Goodnight Jack."

The lid slammed down with a loud bang. Whistling, she went about filling the grave in, taking care to not disrupt the pipe for air. After all, she wouldn't want him to perish too quickly; a drawn-out demise was much more satisfying.

When she was finished, she hefted the shovel across her shoulders and sauntered through her garden, slowly making her way back to the shed. Having disposed of the leftover wine, she carefully gathered the scattered picnic items and loaded them into the bed of her truck. After a final check of the shed door, followed by a long gaze across the gently sloping, green hills, she started the engine and drove home.

CHAPTER 8

AS SHE APPROACHED HER HOUSE, the ever-present cloud of depression descended upon her. She could be in a great mood all day; the moment she turned onto her street, a palpable sadness filled the air, changing everything.

It was a strange phenomenon, considering that it was also the place where she had her best childhood memories.

Her feelings were conflicted. She wanted to leave this house filled with ghosts of the past and start a new life. But she feared that by doing so, she would lose the last vestiges of her humanity, leaving only a cold, empty shell behind.

Someday, she thought, she would make enough money to build a beautiful, sprawling house worthy of the ranch outside of town, with a wrap-around porch and tall windows overlooking her garden. She might even get some cattle and build out a proper ranch, just like her dad always wanted.

As for the little house in town, with its creaking floors and faded wallpaper, it would be entirely remodeled and made into something worthy of her memories—a museum of sorts.

She rolled to a stop in the driveway; the gravel crunching under her tires, and climbed out of the vehicle, pausing for a moment with her chin tilted toward the sky, reveling in the warm sensation of the morning sun on her face.

A long night finally ended, leaving behind a feeling of complete and utter exhaustion. For that matter, the night before was pretty long as well. It takes a lot of energy to prepare the garden, which is why she relegated her gardening for her days off.

Every inch of her body ached. She rubbed her neck and shoulder, doing her best to stretch the muscle. Maybe a hot shower will loosen it up. She glanced down at her hands, noting all the dirt and crusted blood embedded under her fingernails.

Her entire body cried out for sleep. How long had it been this time? Two Days? Had she really not slept for two days? No wonder she made a mistake. She would have to be more cautious in the future. With a yawn and a last stretch, she entered the empty kitchen.

Seeing it now, it was hard to believe that there once was a time when this little room was alive with the aroma of home cooked food, made with love by her Meemaw. How she missed those days. The old woman had some serious culinary skills. Unfortunately, Lori never really picked up on any of them. Now that she was alone, her life was filled with fast food, the occasional date night meal and emptiness.

She strolled into the living room. Sometimes, when her mood was just right, the faint echo of her own giggles would drift back to her, a tangible reminder of those cozy moments long past. The tasty aroma of fresh-baked cookies wafting through the air, mingling with the scent of grease and metal that clung to her father's hair and skin. If only she could travel through time.

She sauntered over to the mantle. These photos used to bring her so much joy, now they reminded her of all she had lost. She lifted the small, black-and-white photo of her grandparents on their wedding day. Their adoration for one another plainly visible in the picture.

As she traced the smiling image of her grandmother, the memory of her infectious laughter and the warm, bright light in her eyes flooded back. With the old man's passing, the light that remained seemed to sigh and die. It was as though a part of her died along with him.

A single tear escaped from the corner of Lori's eye and rolled down her cheek as she recalled the day her Papaw passed.

It was a Saturday afternoon, and he was in the driveway, changing the oil in his truck when he had a heart attack. Meemaw was inside and never knew. It was Lori and her dad who found him.

———

They were returning from a typical happy Saturday of fishing, lunch and the park when they rolled into the driveway. Something in her dad's posture and expression changed subtly, but young Lori was oblivious to the underlying reason.

Pink blotches erupted across his face as the color drained from his skin. He parked his truck, unclipped his belt and with a strange hitch in his voice said, "Okay sweetheart, I'm gonna need you to run on inside and wash up." He lifted her from her seat and placed her on the path. "Go on. Don't dawdle."

With a joyful skip, Lori ran up the path and into the house, the familiar sounds of home washing over her, pausing long enough to hug her Meemaw in the kitchen before running into the bathroom.

When she came out, her entire world was different.

———

She would never forget the sharp, piercing cry that tore from Meemaw's throat as she knelt on the harsh, cold gravel, her body shaking with sobs; Lori's dad sat beside her, equally devastated, Papaw's head resting heavily in his lap. His face pale as ash.

The funeral was somber. It looked like half the town turned out to say their farewell. Everyone knew the old man, he had spent his entire life in this town.

After that, a dark cloud hung heavy over Meemaw. Sure, she tried to pretend as though she was fine, but even Lori, at her young age, knew she wasn't. Losing a soulmate after a lifetime of shared joys and sorrows leaves an ache so deep it feels like a physical wound.

Overnight, the tiny house was quiet, it took quite a bit to get used to. It was like a giant void had opened up and dimmed some of the warmth and light that always seemed to surround them.

Still, the little trio did their best to muddle through and life continued. Happiness returned, at least somewhat, and while there was always something missing, they managed to grow content once again.

That is, until a single, foolish act of trust in a boy changed everything, tearing her life apart in ways she never could have imagined.

CHAPTER 9

SHE COULD LIVE a thousand years and she would never forget how she felt that fateful day, entering the school. The halls were teeming with her classmates. When she approached them, they would stop and stare at her. As she passed, they would huddle together and whisper.

Her heart sank when she laid eyes on her locker. A single word had been scrawled in black marker, Whore. Anxiety washed over her as she turned around and realized that everyone was staring at her. Confused and terrified, she ran for the girl's bathroom and locked herself inside one of the stalls.

The bell rang, but Lori refused to move. In a state of panic, she texted her friends, begging for some explanation.

That was when she learned about the video.

The familiar vibration of her phone signaled a new message—just a link, cold and impersonal, stared back at her. With a trembling finger, she clicked on the link, her heart pounding in her chest.

She gazed down at the tiny screen in her hand. Shock and

horror washed over her as she watched herself in the middle of the most intimate act a man and a woman can share, playing out on the internet for all to see. The room swirled around her as she struggled to catch her breath. She scanned the bottom of the video, over twenty-five thousand views so far.

Oh god!

They had all seen the video.

After recording their private moment without her knowledge, Colter shared the video with the boys, who wasted no time in spreading the gossip to all the girls. Everyone had seen her! The entire school!

She wanted to die. To disappear right then and there.

Why did Colter do this to her? How could he?

Her heart shattered. She trusted him and he did this.

The door to the restroom creaked open. Huddled in the stall, Lori listened to the sound of soft footsteps as they approached, then paused in front of the door.

"Lori?" came the soft, unassuming voice of the school nurse. "Are you okay in there?"

Tears exploded from Lori's eyes. Unable to speak, all she could do was sob.

It took the nurse nearly thirty minutes to coax her from the safety of the stall. Upset and devastated, she couldn't bring herself to look at the judgmental faces of her classmates, so she faked illness and got sent home.

As soon as she closed her bedroom door, she breathed a deep sigh, pressed her back against the door, sunk to the floor and sobbed quietly.

She felt humiliated and dirty. How could he do that? She scraped her memory to see if she could recall him ever setting up the camera. But she could not. He did it all behind her back. Why would he do that?

She pulled her phone from her pocket and fired off a text message to Colter.

Why did you do that?

There was a long, uncomfortable pause, then her phone chimed in response.

Colter: Come on. It ain't no big deal.
    Lori: No big deal? Are you serious? Why did you film it?
    Colter: I thought you'd be okay with it.

She pinched tears from her eyes as her sorrow slowly shifted to anger.

Lori: If you would have asked me, I would have told you it wasn't okay.
    Colter: You should be proud. You look hot in the video.

Anger blossomed into rage.

Lori: You're an asshole! You used me and stabbed me in the back! You had no right to

record me, and you had no right to blast
that damn video all over school.

She stared down at the phone in her hand, listening to the
pound of her own blood in her ears as she waited for a
response.

Colter: Look Lori, I don't get what your
problem is. I was in that video too ya
know.
    Lori: You humiliated me in front of the
entire school!
    Colter: That's how you feel about being
with me? Humiliated? Fine! Maybe we should
break up!

Was he seriously breaking it off with her? What the hell was
happening? No, no, no, no, she was the one who was
supposed to break it off. Who the hell did he think he was?
Her mind was reeling. In her rage, she typed out two words,
Fuck You, then she hit send and tossed the device across
the room.

She spent the rest of the afternoon and evening alone in
her room with her door locked, wishing she could cease to
exist. Both her Meemaw and dad tried, at different times, to
get her to come out, but, feigning sickness, she refused.

Lori didn't return to school the rest of the week.

Of course, she couldn't stay in her bedroom forever, so
after a couple of days, she ventured out into the main part of

the house. She had to admit; she was feeling a lot better when she was around her Meemaw and dad.

Slowly, she began to feel as though things might be okay. It was just one video, and it was only shown to the kids at school. She convinced herself it would blow over and things would go back to normal. To the way, they were before she slept with Colter.

On Sunday night, her phone blew up. Message after message came through from various boys she had never spoken to or even heard of. Some messages were friendly, while others were overtly sexual. Panic seized her as she realized there would be no living this down. With the click of a button, Colter had single handedly ruined her life.

Unable to contain her emotions, once again, she broke down into wracking sobs in her bedroom.

A gentle tap at the door followed the sound of it swinging open. She forgot to lock it behind her.

Her dad stood in the threshold. "Can I come in?" he asked. Without waiting for a response, he came in and sat down on the edge of the bed beside her.

As if things couldn't get any worse, she stared up at him and realized this whole mess would devastate him.

At first, she tried to keep the secret, but when her phone chimed again, she wasn't fast enough to get it before he did.

She'll never forget the look on his face as he read the text.

Unable to hold back any longer, knowing he was going to find out anyway, Lori let loose and told him the whole sordid story. She explained it all, from dates to parties to finally the night she gave her virginity to a boy who only used it for social credit.

Jesse sat silent the whole time. Listening. He asked no

questions and never interrupted her, waiting until the entire story was out.

Exhausted from the purge of emotions she had been struggling with for days, she collapsed against his chest and let him rock her back and forth, all the while stroking her hair.

She lost track of time. Her eyes were swollen and sore, but she had no more tears left to shed. She sat upright and gazed into his eyes.

There was a darkness there she had never seen before.

He flashed a smile that didn't make it to his eyes, then kissed her on the forehead and said, "It's okay. You lay down and rest."

Lori lay back on her bed immediately feeling the call of sleep. "I'm sorry Daddy," she whispered.

"You did nothing wrong sweetheart," he said as he brushed a lock of hair from her face. "Get some rest. It's gonna be okay."

A small part of her wondered if that was possible. How could things ever be okay again? What was done was done. There was no erasing any of it. Even if some miracle happened and the video suddenly disappeared, too many people had already seen it. The internet was forever.

Her dad tucked her in then rose to his feet. "Sweetheart," he said calmly. "This Colter kid, is he the Trask boy?"

She yawned and nodded.

"They got that ranch off the old state road at the edge of town, right?"

She gave another sleepy nod, never once wondering why he needed to confirm that information. Sleep enveloped her. The soothing calm of nothingness carried her away from the turmoil of the past few days.

CHAPTER 10

THE INSISTENT BUZZING of her alarm clock ripped through her sleep, startling her awake. Lori opened her eyes and slowly realized she'd fallen asleep in the living room. She sat up with a groan, raked her fingers through her tangled hair, and rubbed the sleep from her eyes.

She glanced over at the clock; it was time to go to work. With a long exhale, she slowly pushed herself up, gathered her scattered belongings, and after pulling on a pair of sunglasses, walked out to her car.

"You're cutting it close," warned her manager, Todd as she entered the bar.

The heavy wooden door slammed closed behind her, eliminating all signs of the outside world. She scanned the vast, empty bar, the dim lighting highlighting the dust particles dancing in the air. The stench of stale tobacco, rancid liquor and the always present vomit assaulted her nostrils. "I'm here, aren't I?" she asked sarcastically.

She strolled around the back of the bar and placed her bag and phone down. "It's not like you're busy."

He opened his mouth, ready to say something sarcastic,

then shook his head and put the wash rag away. "Just get started doing what I pay you to do."

Lori smirked and placed a hand on her hip. "Pretend this place has customers?"

Tom sighed and gathered his things, then headed for the door. "Don't forget to lock up when you leave tonight." He pulled the door open, filling the dank space with a moment of late afternoon sunlight and fresh air, then left.

Alone at last, Lori glanced around, noting the usuals. Nothing new or exciting. Another full night of popping the caps off bottles of cheap beer. Someday, she told herself, this would all be nothing but a bad dream.

Her phone buzzed. She pressed her finger down on the home button and the screen came to life, highlighting a new message from the dating app. Upon opening the app, she gazed down at the image of a smiling, athletic young man with visible tattoos and muscular arms. So many fuck boys, so little time, she thought as she swiped her finger across the screen.

With a loud creak, the door to the bar opened, letting in a gust of air. She lifted her arm to shield her eyes from the burst of light and watched the newcomer enter. At first she could make out nothing more than a tall, slender silhouette against the yellow glow, when the door finally closed, she could see him more clearly.

A jolt of recognition and shock shot through her as she realized it was the strange man from the bar in Dallas. That's not possible, she thought. She studied him closely, looking for any notable difference between this man and the one from Dallas, hoping this was just a bizarre coincidence, a mere doppelgänger. What are the chances of that happening?

He wore a dark gray suit, complete with a vest and

matching overcoat. The top of his crisp, white button-down shirt peeked out from behind his black tie. Was this some kind of a practical joke? Since when did young men go around looking like extras in a Peaky Blinders episode? With a distinct air of confidence, he strolled up to the bar and took a seat.

Lori placed her phone down behind the counter and readied herself for anything. She made a silent pledge that if this man was law enforcement, she wasn't going to go down easily. She willed herself to be calm, then, resting her hands on the sticky, cool resin surface of the bar, she asked, "What can I do for you?"

The corners of his mouth turned up in a subtle, knowing smile as he regarded her from behind dark, round sunglasses. "Do you have any absinthe?" he asked.

A harsh scoff escaped her lips, and she shook her head. "I think you have us confused." She grinned. "The gay bar is down the street."

A stony silence hung in the air as the strange man stared at her, his face devoid of any expression.

Feeling the sting of her own words, a blush creeping up her neck, Lori cleared her throat and glanced around. "Now come on, you saw the outside of this place. Do we look like the kind of bar you could find absinthe in? Best I can do is a bottle of Jack." She lifted the bottle from the rack and held it up.

"It didn't hurt to ask," he said with a shrug. "Jack, it is." He flashed a playful smile. "I like it neat."

"Somehow I already knew that."

There was an alluring aura about the man, a captivating presence that drew her in. Despite her best efforts, she couldn't quite put her finger on it. Even with his peculiar clothes, the air around him throbbed with a sensual energy.

He moved in a way that told her he understood exactly the effect he had on others—and he enjoyed it.

In a strange, unsettling way, she did too.

Lori shook her head and warned herself not to fall for any of this. No matter how different they first appeared, all men were the same. She poured his drink, the amber liquid swirling in the glass, and then slid it smoothly across the bar toward him.

"Would you like to share one with me?" he asked.

"Far be it from me to pass up a free drink," she said as she poured herself a shot. With one gulp, she downed it, the hot liquid rushing down her throat.

Her phone buzzed; she picked it up and unlocked it to see a message from her latest match.

Hey beautiful.

Filled with hatred, she glared at the words on the screen. All the while, her mind swirled with images of all the ways she could wipe that confident smile off his face.

"Someone's got your full attention I see," said the strange man.

Startled, she glanced up from the screen and found him staring at her. "It's nothing," she replied, shaking her head. After putting the phone down, she poured herself another drink. It was best to not let these men think she was too desperate. Make them wait for a reply. It was far better to play innocent and lead them on; make them believe they were the predators. With the glass raised, she said, "Cheers."

"Cheers," he replied, then he took a sip of his whiskey.

Lori regarded the handsome stranger. "You gonna nurse that all night, or are you here to get drunk?"

A crooked smirk flashed across his face, revealing a set of perfect white teeth. "You're a very straightforward woman. I find it refreshing."

"Uh, huh, that's me, straightforward." She poured another drink and downed it, then slammed the glass down on the bar top.

Once again, her phone chimed. Ordinarily, this would send a current of rage throughout her body, but, thanks to the dulling effect of the liquor, she was numb.

She peered up to find the strange man staring at her.

A sly grin spread across his face. "It appears as though you have a tiny bit of blood on your collar. Did you injure yourself?"

Her hand fluttered to her throat, where her fingers fiddled nervously with her collar. "It's nothing," she replied.

"You know the easiest way to eliminate a blood stain from fabric?" He took a sip from his whiskey, then continued, "Saliva. Yes, nothing dissolves blood better than plain old saliva." He placed his glass down. "The one catch is that it only works for your own blood. Oddly enough, it won't work with someone else's."

As she looked at this strange man, Lori couldn't help but feel like prey. She quickly peeled off her flannel and stuffed it behind the bar, out of sight. Then, pretending she had intended to do that all along, she pulled her hair up into a bun atop her head. A mix of anger and curiosity churned inside her. Was he trying to intimidate her? Who the hell did he think he was? Did he know something?

Unable to contain herself any longer, Lori blurted out, "What's your deal?", her voice tight with frustration. "Are you following me?" She stepped back. "Why did you come here dressed like that? I mean, are you some kind of actor or something?"

"No," he replied, with a shake of his head. "Truth is, I'm just a simple businessman."

"Businessman, huh? Like what? Investment banking or something like that?"

"Actually, I deal in contracts."

"So, what could possibly bring you to this neck of the woods? Last I checked, there ain't a whole lot of big businesses here in this rattrap of a town."

"I'm working on a favor for a longtime friend of mine."

"He must be a good friend for you to come here." She poured herself another drink and held it up. "Well, here's to your business deal. May you get your contract signed."

The man responded, "I'm quite sure I will." He tilted his head. "And thank you."

Once again, she found herself studying him. Her curiosity was piqued. "What's your name, anyway?"

"Les," he replied, holding his hand out.

"Well, Les, I'm pleased to meet you," she said as she took his hand, suddenly shocked at how icy cold it was.

"Pleased to meet you too, Lori."

She pulled her hand free, her fingers tingling from the chill. "How did you know my name?"

Les cocked an eyebrow. "Didn't you tell me?"

She shook her head slowly.

He cleared his throat. "I suppose honesty is the best policy." He sighed. "You, my dear, are the reason I'm here tonight. I have it on good authority that you are a fantastic drummer. My friend would like to make you an offer you cannot refuse."

Startled, Lori didn't quite know how to take what she

was hearing. Suspicion was her first reaction. "Is this some kind of a joke?"

He shook his head. "I'm being quite serious. I assure you."

Once again, curiosity took hold. "Okay, so who is this friend of yours and what does he want with me?"

"He is a renowned musician. He's putting together a band, and you are his drummer of choice."

"Bullshit."

"I assure you, there is no bullshit involved."

As hard as she tried, she could see no sign that he was lying. His offer began to sound appealing. "Why me?"

"Because you are who he wants." He paused and stared at her with an emotionless intensity that made her very uncomfortable. "You have a particular hobby that, without protection, will ultimately end badly for you. It doesn't have to be that way. I can offer you fame, fortune and the freedom to cultivate your garden." He grinned. "Without fear of ever suffering the legal consequences."

The mere mention of her garden sent a wave of anxiety through her, like a sudden alarm blaring in her head. Her heart hammered against her ribs, but she managed a nonchalant scoff. "This is stupid. Nice act though. I gotta hand it to you. I didn't have loser pretending to be a" she paused, unable to find the right word, "whatever it is you're pretending to be, on my bingo card."

"Crossroad demon," he said flatly.

She raised an eyebrow. "Is that what you're calling yourself?"

"It is what I am," he said, his voice low and gravelly, as he removed his sunglasses, revealing blood-red eyes that burned into her.

An icy chill settled over her soul. She shivered. "Nice

contacts," she said, trying desperately to mask her unease. "How much did those set you back?"

He sighed and leaned back against his chair. "I see you will need some convincing." Les glanced around the bar, studying the patrons. "How about this?" He raised his hand in the air and snapped his fingers.

With no provocation, Tank raised his pool cue and brought it down hard atop the head of Sparky. Not to be outdone, the thinner man slammed his full beer bottle against the side of Tank's head. An explosion of beer blasted out, spraying both men.

Unable to move, Lori gaped in shock as Tank grabbed Sparky by the throat and pressed him against the wall.

Panic welled up inside her as she stared on in terror. A primal urge to flee pulsed through her; her mind urged her to run. Like a trapped animal, she nervously glanced at Les, her body tense with anxiety. "Please stop," she choked.

He stared back at her calmly and snapped his finger.

Tank released Sparky, who slumped to the floor, rubbing his neck while he muttered curses under his breath. The larger man stepped back and then abruptly turned and stalked out of the bar.

"Don't be frightened. You are in no danger from me," said Les.

Lori struggled to function against her stark, cold fear as she watched Sparky climb to his feet and disappear into the men's room. Something deep inside her told her she was in mortal danger. "H-How? How d-did you do that?"

"I didn't do anything my dear," he replied. "At least, nothing they hadn't already imagined doing. Trust me when I say those two have been building up to this for a long time. I merely gave them permission to act on their anger."

"What do you want from me?"

"I merely want you to hear me out. To consider my offer."

She quickly made her way back behind the bar as if a strip of wood and cabinets would keep her safe. With trembling hands, she opened the whiskey bottle and lifted it to her mouth. Several gulps later, she wiped her face with the back of her hand and peered up at Les, who was now sitting patiently, waiting.

"This is real," she muttered.

"It most definitely is."

"What if I don't want to accept your offer?"

He bowed his head to her. "Then I shall leave you to your anonymous future."

His words bit deep into her ego. She didn't want to wallow in anonymity for the rest of her life. She was far better than that. The full effect of liquid courage upon her, she locked eyes with him. "So, you're here to ask me to sell my soul?"

He grinned. "My dear, we both know you have already done that." His eyes glowed deep red. "You've already guaranteed your eternal fate. I'm just offering you a chance to capitalize on the transaction for the duration of your earthly existence. I'm here to offer you everything you ever dreamed of."

An icy chill ran down her spine, raising goosebumps on her arms and making her legs tremble. He was speaking the truth. All of this was real. She searched his face for any flicker of deceit, scrutinizing his eyes and the subtle movements of his mouth, but found nothing.

"So, if I accept," she said apprehensively. "What happens next?"

"I bring you to meet him."

"Who? Satan or something?"

He laughed heartily. "You have a wonderful sense of humor. No, my dear. I will take you to meet your new lead singer."

She carefully considered her options. If his words held any truth, her soul was already damned, a chilling realization that left her feeling helpless. Why didn't she feel sad over that? Her mind went over her current body count, reveling in the images of every fuck boy she ever sent to a lonely grave. A wicked grin played across her lips. She gazed up at Les, to find him staring back at her. "If I agree, I get to grow my garden?"

He nodded. "Unhindered and with impunity."

"What if I want more out of the deal? After all, a soul shouldn't come cheap."

Les nodded his head. "I couldn't agree more."

"What guarantees do I have that the man you're speaking of won't turn me away?"

"He's the one who sent me here."

"So, how does he know about me?"

"Suffice to say, he has been watching you for a very long time."

She raised the bottle, the remaining liquid sloshing gently against the glass, and emptied its contents. Fear and doubt washed over her. For the first time in her life, she truly understood the conundrum of the three wishes. She had to choose wisely.

"I'm gonna need a little time to think about this," she said, more than a little afraid of his answer.

"You have twenty-four hours," he replied. "We shall meet again tomorrow evening." He downed what remained of his whiskey, then, with a tip of his hat, he placed his sunglasses over his eyes and slowly strolled out the door, leaving her alone.

An old rock ballad from the seventies played over the speaker. The door to the men's room burst open and Sparky walked out. He gave her a quick nod, then quickly left.

Alone in the empty bar, Lori stared at the door. Her mind reeling as she drank another shot and, with a trembling hand, lit a cigarette.

CHAPTER 11

THE HOURS at work ticked by at a snail's pace. A torrent of questions and worries flooded Lori's mind following the strange encounter. Each possibility heavier than the last. When it was time to close up for the night, she had to force herself to pay attention while she locked up.

When she pulled into her driveway, she suddenly snapped into consciousness and gazed around her, stunned that she was home. She couldn't remember the drive at all.

Making her way into the tiny, dark house, the creak of the floorboards under her feet echoed in the silence as she replayed the night's events in her mind. Drained and exhausted, she let her body fall onto the bed; the springs groaning beneath her weight as she stared up at the empty ceiling. Sleep wouldn't come easily tonight.

If I could have anything in the world? She thought. What would that be?

Of course, there would be one thing—her father.

Was that even possible? Why not? After all, if a girl is gonna sell her soul, shouldn't she get exactly what she demands out of the deal?

Thinking about her father brought a fresh wave of grief, the memory as sharp and painful as a freshly opened wound. One that she carefully tried to avoid poking, but couldn't seem to avoid banging into it all the time.

———

That night, after confessing everything to her father, a deep sense of calm washed over her. Maybe it was the act of purging the nightmare of it all, releasing it into the world, or maybe it was just sitting there, wrapped in the loving arms of her dad—the man who always made her feel safe and loved. For the first time in days, she was able to sleep. Drained of energy and emotionally numb, the world faded as she drifted off into a dreamless sleep.

She awoke the next morning feeling surprisingly peaceful. Sunlight streamed through her curtains, warming her skin with its gentle rays and casting a golden glow across her room. It felt like a typical morning.

But something was off.

She sat up and glanced around her bedroom—nothing was odd or out of place. "Get a grip," she told herself as she ran her fingers through her hair.

After wiping the sleep from her eyes, she climbed out from beneath her cozy covers and padded her way out into the hallway.

The house was silent. How odd. Every morning since she was too small to remember, she awoke to the scent and sound of her grandmother fixing breakfast. On this morning, there was no savory scent of bacon or sausage. No sound of dishes moving around in the kitchen. In fact, there was no indication that anyone was home.

Apprehension took hold. Slowly, she made her way down the tiny hall, into the living room.

It was empty.

The ominous silence that surrounded her sent a shiver down her spine. Where was everyone?

"Meemaw?" she said aloud, afraid to round the corner into the kitchen.

Seconds ticked by—there was no response.

"Dad?"

Silence.

An icy dread seized her, making her heart pound in her chest. Something was terribly wrong; she could feel it in her bones.

She inhaled a deep breath and took a full step forward into the kitchen.

The room was empty and cold—two things it had never been in her life. Even when she was feeling unwell or quite sick, Meemaw made sure there was coffee in the pot and breakfast on the table. But on this particular day, there was neither.

A deep sense of dread threatened to swallow her whole. She wrapped her arms around herself and shivered.

Maybe Meemaw slept in, thought Lori. Or she might not be feeling well.

She peeked around the corner at her grandmother's door. It seemed so lifeless. Come to think of it, that was how the entire house felt.

But what about her father? Where was he? A very big part of her didn't want to know the answer to that question.

When she grew too old to share a bedroom with him, he moved his things into the tiny garage. Papaw and Meemaw wanted to build another room on the house, but her dad countered by insisting they save their money. After all, it wouldn't be long before he could save enough to build a proper home on the land. Besides, he told them; he preferred to sleep near his kit. That way he could stay up late and not worry about waking anyone. After all, he was a night owl.

Of course, the way things go, the years passed, and nothing changed. The tiny house remained the same as it always was and her father continued to sleep in the little garage, just him, a single bed, his drum kit, a window banger for the summer, and a small space heater for those cold winter nights.

Lori peeked out the kitchen window, hoping to see the faint glimmer of a light through the tiny window of the garage. Nothing.

He had to be out there. Determined to prove to herself that she was being paranoid, she pulled open the door and stepped outside.

Golden sun splashed over her, the rays warm on her skin, yet she felt no warmth.

She stared at the garage, afraid to take a step forward. That was when she heard the car's engine purring. She moved her gaze to the driveway and found herself staring through the windshield at her Meemaw.

Her face, red and swollen, suggested she'd been crying. Upon seeing Lori, her face crumpled, and she dissolved into a torrent of tears.

Lori ran to the vehicle, flung open the door, and wrapped her arms around her grandmother. She had no idea what had her Meemaw so upset, but she was sure, at that moment, that nothing in her life would ever be the same.

"Meemaw," she whispered. "What's wrong?"

Slowly, deliberately, the old woman pulled back, her

eyes lingering on Lori's face. She moved her head slowly from side to side, all the while, tears continued to stream down her cheeks.

The lack of forthcoming answers was taking its toll. A sudden, sharp pang of irritation hit her, along with a terrifying sense that the truth would be too much to bear. But she had to know.

"Meemaw?" she said. "What's going on? Where's dad?"

As soon as she mentioned her father, the old woman broke down again.

The memory of the day her grandpa died came rushing back. Her grandmother had the same look in her eyes.

Something snapped inside Lori. She ran to the garage, the rising panic tightening her chest as she flung open the side door with a desperate heave.

The room was empty. The small bed in the corner, where her father slept for years, looked untouched. She spun around and ran back to the car.

"Meemaw, please," she cried. "I'm begging you to tell me what is going on."

The old woman wiped her face, then climbed out of the vehicle. She reached out a trembling hand to Lori. Gazing into her eyes, she said, "Your daddy has done something terrible."

———

Laying on her bed, Lori wiped the tears from her cheeks and sat up. Even now, the muscle memory of the pain and heartache she felt that day remained as strong as if it were only happening now.

Flashing back, she remembered her grandmother's

description; her father, after closing her bedroom door, walked with purpose to the kitchen and gathered his keys.

Her Meemaw tried to talk to him, but his thoughts were elsewhere. He said nothing to her when he left.

Three hours later, the phone rang. It was Jesse, calling from the town jail. He had gone to the Trask home where he confronted the boy's father. A fight broke out between them that ended with Colter's father unconscious on the garage floor.

The boy and his mother tried to hide inside the house and wait for the police to arrive, but Jesse would not be deterred. He kicked the door in and after a brief chase through the house; he managed to get hold of Colter, and beat the teenager until he was an unconscious heap of bruises, broken bones, and blood.

When the police arrived, Lori's father surrendered—there was no more fight left in him. He was brought to jail and he would remain there until his hearing.

Apart from a few bruises, some stitches, and a wounded pride, Colter's father was fine after he woke up. But Colter—he remained in a coma for three months.

The trial was swift, as Jesse never once tried to fight the charges. Even though many men in the town agreed with his actions, it simply wasn't enough. The judge was a friend of the Trask family. In the end, he sentenced Lori's father to twenty years for assault and attempted murder.

Everything in her life went from worse to horrible.

The relentless staring and whispering from her classmates left Lori feeling too ashamed to return to school. With no other options, her grandmother decided to home-school her for the rest of her schooling.

She spent her days alone with her Meemaw, refusing to go outside. At night, she would venture out into the cramped garage and pound away on the drums until she had no strength left, only to return inside and collapse on her bed. On Saturdays, she and her grandma would drive the two hours south to visit her father in prison.

That was her life until she turned eighteen, and the old woman insisted she go out and find a job.

After that, things were okay for a little while, at least, they became a new normal. Then, one day, the inevitable happened and her Meemaw passed, leaving Lori alone in her misery.

CHAPTER 12

THE FULL WEIGHT of this decision rested heavy on her mind. She had to admit; it was tempting to jump right in, but the chance to get more out of the deal was something she found irresistible. Her head swimming with possibilities, she put on her boots, grabbed her keys and made the two-hour drive to see her father.

The guards all knew her by name. They were always nice to her, in fact, over the years, many had taken the time to let her know that, in their eyes, her father was a hero for what he did. They respected him.

Most of the other prisoners considered Jesse a hero. He was a good man, doing what any other father would have done for his daughter.

Her father, with his warm smile and easy laugh, was a likable man who quickly earned the respect of those around him. That's part of the reason it was so hard to understand why he had never found another woman to marry. In the end, Lori had concluded that the reason he never found a woman to be with was because they didn't have anything financial to offer.

Yet another reason this deal was so tempting.

With a quick nod of his head and a wide smile, the guard hit the buzzer and let her enter the visiting room.

The cold, sterile setting always made her skin crawl. Her dad was an outdoorsman, the thought of him corralled by these drab, concrete walls made her sad. She knew he much preferred being by the water, watching the sunrise, listening to the gentle sound of waves lapping at the shore. That's where he belonged.

Her father stood by her when she was nothing more than a burden on his young life. Rather than run away from it all, he stayed and cared for her. This was a stark contrast to her mother.

She remembered the one and only time she had ever spoken to the woman, if you could call it speaking.

———

It was shortly after her nineteenth birthday.

Lori had thought the pain of the past few years was behind her, at least the majority of it. It was impossible, after all, to move on completely when she had to visit her father in prison every week.

She had just finished a grueling shift, pulling double duty in the kitchen at the small diner at the edge of town. It wasn't much, but the greasy little establishment was the only place that was willing to hire her at the time.

When she rolled into the driveway, an eerie sense of déjà vu settled upon her as she stared at the dark little house. This was not normal. Her grandmother would still be up, she always waited for Lori to return home safely before going to bed. There would be lights on.

But on this night, there were none.

Knowing all too well what she would find, Lori climbed the step to the back door and entered the house.

The icy chill of death was all around her.

She clicked on the light in the kitchen, then walked slowly into the living room. The bright light from the kitchen cast a cold glow on the room, illuminating all she needed to see.

Her grandmother sat in the old chair by the fireplace, a dog-eared book resting on the floor at her feet. Eyes wide open, the old woman stared at nothing at all.

Hot tears streamed down Lori's face, blurring her vision as she stumbled across the room. The old woman was cold to the touch. Sobbing, Lori gently closed her eyes and kissed her on the forehead. "I love you Meemaw," she whispered.

She knew the procedure, but she wasn't quite ready to do it, so she collapsed to the floor and sat at the feet of the old woman and sobbed.

Three days later, the funeral was held. Following the Colter incident, most townsfolk shunned her family, their cold stares and hushed whispers a constant reminder of their ostracism. So, unlike her grandfather's funeral, her grandmother's was a silent and lonely affair.

For two hours, Lori sat alone by the casket. She was alone now. No one would be there to greet her when she came home at night. Her life was a joke.

The sound of dirt hitting the coffin echoed as she stood by the grave, the smell of freshly turned soil heavy in the air. Lori didn't want to go home. The house was lifeless; it was far too painful to be there.

The crew had finished their work and collected all the chairs and equipment, then left, leaving her alone, kneeling on the ground. With the sound of birds chirping in the distance, Lori broke down and sobbed.

The hours slipped by as she cried until she had no more tears. She glanced around her, realizing it was dark.

With a final goodbye to her Meemaw, Lori rose to her feet, wiped her hands off on her pants, then slowly made her way back to her truck and the old house.

Sitting in the driveway, gazing out at the dark little house, Lori wasn't sure she could handle being inside. She decided to spend the night in the garage.

Since he had been in prison, Lori could never bring herself to remove her dad's things. Instead, she chose to keep it all exactly the way it was on the last night he was home, just in case a miracle would happen and he would be released.

She plopped herself heavily on the small bed and wiped a small trickle of a tear from her cheek. This was her life now. She had no one left.

An old picture of her and her dad sat on the table beside the bed. He was such a handsome young man, holding his toddler on his lap, smiling at the camera. According to everyone who knew him back then, he was destined for great things, but it was impossible to live the life of a professional musician when one had an infant to care for.

No matter how she parsed it out, she couldn't help but come to the conclusion that all she had ever done for the man was ruin his life—to steal his dreams and grind them to dust.

Lori swiped a thumb across the glass, yearning for the ability to go back in time, but knowing that was impossible.

A thought suddenly occurred to her. Her mother was still alive. Or, at least, that's what she believed. She remembered some time ago, not long after her father went to prison, her grandmother had given her a slip of paper with a name and phone number on it. She said it was her mother.

At the time, Lori had no interest in talking to the woman who had abandoned her when she was a baby, so she stuffed the paper in a drawer in her desk and never gave it a moment's thought again.

That paper was calling to her.

What did she have to lose? She climbed to her feet and walked into the house, turning on every light as she went. In her bedroom, she pulled open the drawer and after a moment of rooting around, found the slip of paper.

She stared at the numbers for a long time. What was she going to say? What does one say in a moment like this? Hello, it's your daughter, Lori. You deserted me when I was a newborn. Do you remember me?

Brushing her thoughts aside, she entered the number, then, holding her breath, waited.

It rang four times, making Lori consider hanging up. It's probably not her number any longer, she told herself.

Suddenly, the ringing stopped. The silence on the other end was unnerving.

"Hello?" said a gruff voice that sounded as though it had been awakened from slumber.

Glancing at the clock, she realized it was well past midnight. Oh god! How could she be so stupid to call in the middle of the night? It was too late to go back now, she cleared her throat and responded, "Um." Her throat was so dry, she licked her lips and tried to swallow, but that only made it worse.

What was she supposed to call this woman? Mom? That felt wrong.

"Who is this?" came the voice, ringing with irritation.

"Um, this is Lori," she said. "Lorelai." She closed her eyes and berated herself for being so stupid.

"What do you want from me?" demanded the woman on the other end. Her tone was harsh and cold.

"I-I don't know," said Lori. "I-I'm sorry to bother you."

"Then don't," said the woman.

Lori sat stunned. The woman's tone and words stung as though an invisible hand had slapped her across the face. Tears streamed down her cheeks as her phone screen went black.

What did you think was gonna happen? She asked herself. Did you think she was gonna be happy to hear from you? That she would wrap her arms around you and say, "Oh don't worry my dear, Momma's here."

You're a fool! A helpless, lonely fool. No one can love you because you're a loser.

She cried out and hurled her phone across the room, where it smashed against the wall and dropped to the floor. Sobbing with a mixture of rage and heartache, she sunk to the floor.

———

A loud buzz disrupted her thoughts, causing her to jump in her seat. No matter how many times she had been in this very room, surrounded by the sights, scents and sounds of the prison, Lori could never get used to that sound.

On the other side of the room, the door clicked open with a sharp metallic sound, and a guard, his footsteps heavy on the polished floor, escorted her dad into the room and over to the table. As soon as Jesse's eyes fell upon her, they lit up with that familiar, bright light that was always there when he looked at her.

His age was showing, etching lines into his face and whitening his hair. The young man was gone, replaced by an older man whose face was testament to years of hardship and disappointment. He didn't look well.

"Hey sweetie," he said as he took a seat and held her hand. "How ya doin'?"

"I just wanted to visit," she said.

A look of concern swept across his face. "Is everything okay?"

She nodded. "Oh, it's great. Or at least it's all the same. I'm doing good."

"All the same, huh?" He leaned back in his chair. "You look good. Like the world is treating you better."

The offer came to her mind. "I had an offer to join a band," she blurted.

His face lit up. "That's wonderful! What's the name?"

"I don't know that yet. A representative of the band came by and invited me to join. He said I was the exact sort of drummer they wanted."

"A representative," said her father. "Like a manager?"

"Yeah, I think that would be what he's called."

"How do you know this is legit?"

Because he's a demon, she thought. There was no way she could say that to him, so she made up a story on the spot. "It's okay, Dad. They're legit. I already looked into it."

A look of relief washed over his face. "That's good to know. So, tell me about this band. What sort of music?"

It suddenly occurred to her she had no idea. She couldn't make something up, because if she was wrong, she would look like a liar. She decided that pretending to keep it a secret would be best. "You're gonna have to wait to find out," she said, flashing a smile.

"I guess I have no other choice," he said with a wink. "I look forward to seeing you on the cover of Billboard."

The cover of Billboard, now that would be incredible,

she thought. Leaving the band to rest, she diverted the conversation to their typical discussion about day-to-day things.

When she left the prison, she knew, without a doubt, that she would accept the offer on one condition. Her father would be released.

With a skip in her step and a light feeling in her heart, Lori walked across the parking lot to her car. She pulled out the card with Les's number and dialed.

It took less than a full ring before he picked up.

"Lorelai," came his voice, silky and confident. "Am I to assume you have made a decision?"

"Yes," she replied. "But I have some conditions. Where can we meet?"

THE MOON HUNG heavy in the inky sky, its pale light casting long, distorted shadows across the eerie landscape. She pulled out her phone and double checked to make sure this was where Les told her to meet him. A crossroads in the middle of nowhere, surrounded by nothing. Just her, a gravel road, two street signs and an old tree. How fitting.

The temperature was warm, but Lori couldn't shake the icy chill that seemed to permeate her entire body. Pulling her hoodie tight, she zipped it all the way up and shoved her hands deep into the pockets.

Was this the right thing to do? She wondered. Yes. Yes, it was. For as long as she could recall, all she ever wanted was to be a famous drummer for a famous band. Until now, that dream was nothing more than fantasy.

She was standing at the precipice of achieving every-thing she only ever dared to daydream about. Now was not the time to waver or even question.

But will it hurt? She wondered.

"Who cares," she said aloud. "If it hurts, it'll be momen-tary. You'll get over it. It's a small price to pay to finally live the life you were meant to live. Get it together, girl. Don't pass this up."

The sound of an engine rumbling stole her attention. From her perch on top of the car, she watched as a single headlight approached, filling her with a mixture of anticipation and apprehension. The motorcycle rolled to a stop beside her, then the engine cut off. Wearing a wild grin, Les climbed off the bike.

"Shouldn't you be wearing a helmet?" asked Lori.

"Why? There's no need. Besides, there really is nothing quite like the sensation of wind rushing through your hair while a mechanical beast rumbles beneath your body."

He pulled off his leather gloves and laid them on the tank.

"Then why the gloves?"

"I like the feel of leather against my skin." He stepped closer. "Okay, my young friend," he said. "Are we ready?"

"Wait!" she blurted as she hopped off the hood of her car. "I have a few conditions."

Les nodded, staring at her with calculating eyes. "Go on."

She cleared her throat. "First, I want to make sure this is all real."

"I assure you, this is all very real. You will be rich and famous beyond your wildest imagination."

The icy sensation that chilled her soul told Lori he wasn't lying. This was very real. She continued, "I want to be an integral part of the band. Not just the drummer. I want to be a part of everything."

"He would have it no other way," said Les.

"I'm not just going to go along with everything. I want to have a say in how things happen."

His blood-red eyes blinked slowly. "You will have as much of a say as he decides is necessary."

Lori wasn't sure she liked that answer, but she knew Les was being honest with her. She also understood there would be some concessions. "That will have to do," she said.

"Is there more?" he asked.

"Yes, two more things."

"Let's have them."

Her voice caught, a painful lump formed in her throat as she struggled, stunned by the difficulty of speaking the name aloud. It occurred to her that she hadn't said his name in years. "Colter Trask," she croaked. "I want him."

A wicked grin played across the demon's lips. "My lady, you have a real dark streak. How would like him? Alive and kicking or flayed and carved into pieces?"

"I want him alive. I want him to suffer at my hands. When the time is right, I will tell you to bring him to me."

"Oh, you are a dark one," cooed Les. "Consider it done." His face became serious. "And your final demand?"

She licked her lips. "I want my father out of prison." Something in his face made her uneasy.

"My dear, I'm not a miracle worker."

"No," she said forcefully. "You're a demon. You can make anything happen."

"It's not so simple," he said. "I would have to manipulate an entire government apparatus. Do you have any idea how absolutely devoid of humanity bureaucrats are?"

"This isn't a request," she said. "I don't care how difficult it is."

He stared at her for an uncomfortably long time.

Lori held her ground, fighting the urge to look away, with her back straight, she stared back at him, refusing to be the first to break eye contact.

Les sighed and spun around. Walking in tight circles, he tapped his chin thoughtfully, the rhythmic tap-tap-tap echoing as he muttered, "I suppose there might be an avenue or two where I could wheedle in and pull some strings." He stopped and stared down at the ground as though he were reading, then abruptly spun around to face Lori.

"Okay," he said. "Your father's freedom will be guaranteed." He held up a hand. "But you will have to allow me a fortnight to get it done."

She had no idea how long a fortnight was, but she wasn't willing to ask him for fear of showing any weakness.

"As long as it's done," she said.

He nodded. "I assure you it will be."

With the deal finally done, she ran her fingers through her hair, feeling the strands stick to her sweaty scalp, and wiped her clammy palms on her thighs. "Okay," she said. Excited for what the future would unfold, she locked eyes with Les. "I'm ready to meet him."

Before she could finish the words, Les snapped his fingers.

A MUMENT LATER, they were standing at the base of a set of stone steps.

"Where are we?" she asked as she glanced around, disoriented.

"You're new home."

"I already have a home," she replied harshly. "I didn't ask for a new one."

Without missing a beat, Les nodded his head in agreement. "Then let's refer to this as your new base of operations."

Lori stared at him, his expression unreadable, trying to figure out whether he was being genuine or sarcastic. Unable to discern which it might be, she changed the subject. A glance around revealed crumbling buildings with broken windows, overgrown weeds pushing through cracks in the pavement, and the eerie silence that spoke of long desertion. They were in some town and by the looks of it, there were no residents.

She shifted her gaze to the building that loomed large

before her at the top of the steps. "Is this a church?" she said aloud.

Les grinned. "You could say it is, though, it's unlike any you have seen before." He gestured for her to follow as he climbed the steps.

A deep sense of unease washed over her, but she brushed it aside and followed him up the stairs and across the threshold.

A vast room opened before her, the soaring ceiling a breathtaking expanse of aged copper tiles, gleaming faintly in the dim light. The rustic white walls were punctuated every two feet by large, colorful stained-glass windows, each a gruesome depiction of carnage and death. A row of worn wooden pews lined both sides of the aisle, leading to a stage at the far end. The air was filled with the sweet sounds of a beautiful melody as a lone figure sat at a polished piano, his fingers moving effortlessly across the keys. Her body swooned. She closed her eyes, the music washing over her as she swayed, filling her mind with horrific images of blood and torture.

The music stopped.

Opening her eyes, she watched the man rise and slowly walk over to her, his shadow stretching long and eerie across the floor. He paused and gazed down at her.

Tall—he was so tall. The man's slender, muscular frame loomed over her, casting a shadow that felt both intimidating and strangely alluring. The air hung heavy with the scent of burnt embers. She gazed up at his face. His eyes were two pitch black orbs, surrounded by a spiderweb of black veins that reached out toward his thick, dark brown hair.

Lori licked her dry lips as she stared in awe.

"My dear," said Les. "Allow me to introduce you to Ten.

Also known as Ratten Koenig, or, in English, The Rat King."

The tall man leaned forward and nodded his head. He took her hand in his. "I am very happy to see you. Is it safe to assume you have accepted our offer?"

Unable to speak, a tiny, hesitant nod was the only response she could manage.

Ten's lips curled into a beautiful smile, revealing a row of perfectly white teeth. She couldn't help but notice his abnormally long canines, their sharp points glinting in the light, contributing to his unsettling, animalistic presence. He moved his hand in a circular motion, in a silent command.

The wind whipped and swirled around her, a chaotic dance of dust and debris stinging her face. She squinted her eyes and watched as a plume of rainbow tinted smoke churned at her feet. A sinuous shape slithered deep inside the cloud. She gazed in, trying to discern what it might be. A serpent. A sleek serpent, its scales shimmering with iridescent light, was hidden among the wispy colors; its red eyes glowed ominously.

The snake slithered around her entire body, hissing and pulsating. The creature's soft, cool skin, like velvet, brushed against hers. She felt no fear—only elation. Her pulse quickened.

The creature rose until its eyes met hers, the gaze piercing and unsettling, making her feel exposed and vulnerable.

"*Thurisaz,*" hissed the serpent.

The word lodged itself in Lori's mind, a dark seed taking root among her thoughts and memories, twisting and growing. She didn't know what it meant, but she didn't care.

Through the cloud of smoke, Lori locked eyes with Ten. She had no fear.

A searing, fiery pain shot through her right arm, making her gasp. Glancing down, she watched, mesmerized, as a strange symbol burned itself into her forearm, the heat intense and sharp. A single line with a pointy thorn jutting out from the center. The smell of burnt flesh permeated the air.

Her skin felt like it was burning, the heat radiating through her bones. A frantic rhythm pounded in her chest, her heart threatening to burst free from its confines. Unable to breathe, Lori collapsed to her knees.

With the cloud's dissipation, the snake vanished, leaving behind only the cloying, sickeningly sweet smell of burnt flesh. Feeling woozy, a wave of nausea washed over her as she shook her head and touched her arm, her fingers tracing the strange symbol, wondering about its meaning.

Ten held out his hand for her.

Without hesitation, she reached out, her fingers brushing against his as she accepted his support. Rising to her feet, she gazed adoringly into his deep, black eyes, noticing the way the light glinted off their surface. A strange energy thrummed through her, a potent life force she'd never known, as the realization that she would die for this man settled in her bones.

A warm, calming sensation washed over her. For the first time in years, she felt a deep sense of belonging. Staring up at this handsome, dark stranger, she felt nothing but love for him. He accepted her for who she was and in return wanted nothing more than to have her by his side, doing what she was born to do—play the drums.

The corners of his lips curled into a wicked grin, his

eyes gleaming with mischief as he twirled a strand of her hair around his finger.

It was pure white. She reached up and ran her fingers through her hair, pulling it forward. It seemed as though the rest of her hair remained the same as always, except for the single white streak.

A strange tingling sensation, like a thousand tiny ants, crawled up her arm. With a delicate finger, she traced the symbol that was now permanently embedded in her skin. "What does this mean?" she asked, not really expecting an answer, so she wasn't surprised when none came.

What's done is done, she thought.

From a far corner of the church, a shadowy figure emerged, its movements slow and deliberate. Its stiff limbs, crackling and popping with each movement, jerked in a way that mimicked a marionette's dance. It came closer and stopped alongside Ten.

It was a girl. Or at least it appeared to be a girl. With a sharp tilt of her head, she stared at Lori, her dark eyes unwavering and cold. Something in its posture, the way it moved, the glint in its eyes, spoke of an inherent, deeply unsettling wickedness. Lori wanted it gone from her sight.

She glanced over at Les, noticing his uneasy stare fixed on the creature, a mirror of her own apprehension. For some reason, this did nothing to allay Lori's feelings, rather it only served to make her even more uneasy. If a demon was ill at ease around this thing, it had to be bad.

Doing her best to avoid eye contact with the thing, she moved her gaze over to Ten.

He leaned close, whispering to the creature. A creepy giggle echoed back, and with a series of sickening pops and cracks, it turned, ambled to the stage, and disappeared behind a set of heavy, black curtains. It returned a moment later, carrying something in its hands.

With a deep bow, the creature presented a set of drumsticks to Ten.

He took them gently in his hand and nodded to the girl.

Her head popped and jerked in Lori's direction, her eyes full of malevolence, her lips pulled into the creepiest grin Lori had ever seen. "Welcome," she said with a raspy voice, then she turned and walked back into the shadows.

Ten held out the set of drumsticks and asked quietly, "Are we ready to begin?"

The longer she gazed into his dark eyes, the safer she felt. A wicked grin played across her lips as she took hold of the sticks and turned to face him. She gazed up at him with adoring eyes. "Yes."

AFTER LORI STEPPED out of the shower, she noticed he had already left. The bed still bore the indentation of his body. Walking over, she ran her hand over the spot, sensing a lingering warmth.

The room smelled of burnt embers, a scent that clung to his skin like a shroud. The sound of a distant car honking outside, echoed through the window, mixing with the muffled sounds of a TV show playing in the adjacent hotel room. She stared at the bed, feeling the familiar ache in her chest. Why was it always like this? Why did he always leave like this? And more importantly, why did she tolerate it?

This so-called relationship—if one could even call it that —was a laundry list of everything she despised: the emotional distance, the pervasive sense of dread. The lone-liness. Yet, here she was, a ready, willing and able participant.

A soft chuckle escaped her lips. "Situation-ship from hell," she muttered to herself. "Fitting."

When she first met them, she had no idea things were as complicated as they were. But, slowly over time, she came to realize that Ten and Mason are two distinct individuals sharing the same vessel.

Her attraction was immediate, drawn like a moth to a flame, it took her months before she realized it was Mason who captivated her. As for Ten, he was an enigma. A quiet figure shrouded in an air of mystery. Her respect for him mingled with a strange sort of attraction, but that was as far as her feelings for him went.

He was the bandleader—the unseen hand guiding their every move. Like a puppeteer, his insidious influence pushing them toward a mysterious goal only he understood.

Mason, on the other hand, was the heart and soul of it all. She was convinced that, without him, there would be no band. His artistry was a visceral expression of his heartache and pain. His music had a poignant impact; every note resonated deep within your soul. It was impossible to ignore.

Gazing at her reflection in a mirror, Lori touched the side of her neck. A soft sigh escaped her lips. The memory of his kiss lingered. Closing her eyes, she felt the soft pressure of his lips, a phantom touch against her skin.

A sudden chill swept through the room as the air shifted, raising goosebumps on her arms. She was no longer alone.

Over the past year, Lori came to know this sensation all too well. She turned to find the creepy black-eyed child, Riley, standing in the doorway.

The creature, its eyes unfocused, ignored her as it stared at the empty bed, her head cocked slightly, a silent question in her posture.

A deep sense of revulsion, as though she were looking at something spawned in hell, always accompanied the sight of

Riley, and Lori wondered if she'd ever overcome that feeling.

She cleared her throat and asked, "What is it?"

Riley turned and locked eyes with her. A chilling malevolence, cold and sharp as shards of ice, glittered behind the girl's eyes. A long, uncomfortable silence hung in the air as she stared, then her lips curled into a grotesque, chilling smile. "I've come to see if you need any assistance in preparing for the show this evening."

The thought of this thing touching her with its icy hands sent a shudder down Lori's spine. She shook her head. "I've got it. You can go help the others." She pulled the towel tight around her as if a fluffy piece of fabric could protect her. "When is the van getting here to take us to the venue?"

"Thirty minutes," replied Riley.

"Has Ten already left?"

"Yes," she replied. With a flurry of wet snaps and pops, Riley slowly moved her head and then her eyes back over to the bed.

A heavy, suffocating silence descended, thick with unspoken tension.

From the moment she first laid eyes on Riley, Lori was repulsed by her bizarre, almost puppet-like movements. Of the band members, only Mason seemed truly at ease with her presence; Lori sensed a palpable tension from the others. Even Les seemed to do his best to avoid interacting with her as much as possible.

As for Ten, he seemed to stiffen when she was around. Oddly enough, the little girl with the demonic, black eyes seemed to be the one thing that made him uncomfortable.

She knew the story of how the creature known as Riley came to be. It didn't help. No matter how she tried,

Lori could never overcome her revulsion. Riley was unnatural.

On the upside, the black-eyed girl's presence was a sure-fire way to determine who was in control of the vessel at the moment. If Mason was in control, and she appeared, his demeanor would visibly shift from guarded to openly relieved, and his step would become lighter. However, if Ten was in control when Riley appeared, his entire body tensed, a clear sign of his discomfort at her presence. Such a strange phenomenon, considering they shared the same body, yet their minds and emotions were completely separate.

For the most part, Lori tried her best to accept Riley and be kind, but the girl's dark eyes and unsettling aura filled her with a deep, chilling dread. Not to mention, more than once, she swore she caught Riley's hateful glare burning into her, making the hairs on the back of her neck stand on end. Perhaps she disapproved of Lori and Mason's relationship.

Whatever the reason, Lori had the distinct impression that Riley disliked her. To be honest, Lori felt the same way.

Riley's head snapped toward Lori with a sickening jerk, her gaze cold and unnerving.

"Is there something else you want?" asked Lori, trying to sound aloof as opposed to scared, which was how she was really feeling at that moment.

"I'll go now and see if the others need help," said Riley. Without another word, the ghastly creature, accompanied by the sound of snapping bones, left the room, pulling the door closed behind her.

Lori slowly let out her breath, the tension leaving her body as she realized she'd been holding it. Her phone chimed, an oddly cheerful jingle cutting through her unease. She picked it up from the nightstand to read Les's message. A limo would arrive in thirty minutes to take her and the others to the venue.

Tonight was the biggest night of their career. They were about to perform in front of the largest audience they had ever played before. The venue was massive—the crowd would be equally so. This is it. All their hard work had come to this moment.

Images of blood-splattered floors and headless bodies, the crime scenes Detective Reyes had shown her, flooded her mind. She brushed them aside—their music had nothing to do with any of that. It wasn't their fault that some teenagers went feral and murdered their whole family. Contrary to what the detective believed, their music was filled with messages of beauty and love. There was no hidden malevolent undertone.

Lori was, however, more than a little surprised that the detective never inquired about Colter. She must not have been that great of a detective to not connect the dots.

With a shrug of her shoulders, Lori swiftly dressed, setting her focus on the day ahead.

Today, all her dreams will come true.

Arriving at the venue, she gasped; the sheer scale of the building was breathtaking, dwarfing everything around it. Peering out through the dark-tinted windows of the limo, the muffled sounds of the crowd reached her ears as her eyes scanned the throng of young people gathered all along the perimeter of the building. Wearing sweatshirts, t-shirts, and hats adorned with the band's logo, they screamed, waving frantically as the limo appeared. Lori waved back; an insignificant gesture lost against the reflective, dark tint of the glass.

The vehicle slid down the narrow delivery dock lane and through a set of garage doors that closed behind them.

As she emerged from the limo, Lori scanned the vast open space. She wanted to revel in every moment—every sensation. This was her lifelong dream come true.

Les sauntered up, the corners of his mouth turned up in his usual grin. "Gentlemen, and my lady," he said with a tilt of his head. "If you will follow Riley, she will show you to your dressing room." With a flourish, he stepped away, heading for a side door. "I'll be back shortly."

The sound of the door swinging open echoed around the vast space as sunlight poured in from outside. A moment later, it slammed closed with a loud bang, leaving Lori and the others in Riley's hands.

Lost in a world of daydreams, Lori quickly got ready, barely noticing the mundane tasks. When she was ready, a stage manager, clipboard in hand, briskly ushered them down a narrow hallway to the main suite where Ten was waiting.

Gazing down through the window at the enormous crowd of young people, Ten said, "I can feel them. Their blind adoration and pure devotion is intoxicating. Tonight is only the beginning."

Something about those words made Lori's skin crawl.

A sharp tap on the door was followed by the frantic rush of feet as the stage manager bustled in, a whirlwind of nervous energy. It was time. Twirling her drumsticks in her hands, Lori waited until the others had gone, then she walked alongside Ten to the stage.

AFTERWORD

Welcome to part two.

As you can undoubtedly know by now, this is no typical, run of the mill band. You might even have an image forming in your mind of what is to come.

Feel free to drop me a line and share your thoughts. I'd love to hear.

What you just read was the second installment in the four part collection of origin stories for our distinct set of characters.

We're halfway there. Once everyone has had a chance to meet all the members of the band, the real fun will begin.

If you enjoyed this story, please be sure to leave a rating or
review.